THE PARIS PUZZLER

LOL Detective Club Book #2

By E.M. FINN

LOL DETECTIVE CLUB BOOK 2: THE PARIS PUZZLER

First Edition, May 2016

Cover Illustration by Steven Bybyk and Natalie Khmelvoska
Cover Design by EMF

Table of Contents

CHAPTER ONE

Lottie Parker fell flat on her face as the train car lurched to a stop. "Paris Metro Station," a voice over the loudspeaker said in a thick French accent.

"That's our stop," her big brother, Oliver, or Ollie for short, shouted as he stood up in the train car aisle.

Ollie was ten years old. His two younger sisters, Lottie and Lucy, were both eight and a half years old. Lottie and Lucy were identical twins who looked so much alike even their dad got them confused.

"This isn't our train stop, Ollie," Lottie said, as she climbed back into her seat. "We have three more stations to go."

"There's no use arguing. Just ask Dad, he'll know," Lucy said.

Mr. Parker, their dad, was checking his cell phone a few rows down. He had a map of the Paris metro route unfolded on his lap, and his camera bag was stowed neatly at his feet. Mr. Parker worked as a photojournalist for an important magazine. His job was to take photos of some of the most interesting places in the world.

His three children, Ollie, Lucy, and Lottie often traveled with him, and they got to see the best places in the world. It also meant that they spent a lot of time hanging out on planes and trains, traveling to the next exciting location.

This week, they were staying in Paris,

France, where their dad was photographing a special Picasso Exhibit at the Louvre Art Museum in Paris, France. Pablo Picasso was an important artist who lived in the 1900s. He started an art movement called Cubism.

Lottie opened the guide book about Paris she had pulled out of her backpack.

"It says here that the Louvre Art Museum is home to the Mona Lisa. You know, the painting of the woman with the mysterious smile," she read aloud.

Lucy leaned in close as Lottie showed her a picture of the painting.

"The Mona Lisa was stolen over a hundred years ago from the museum. Good news, they caught the guy," Lucy said as she read the next page of her book.

"I wonder who stole it?" Ollie mumbled as he played Minecraft on his tablet.

"Well, some people thought Picasso stole it," Lottie said. "But it turned out it was a worker at the museum. It was a mystery for two whole years before they caught him."

"Did you say mystery?" Lucy exclaimed. "You know how much I love detective stuff. Maybe we'll solve our own case while we're at the museum."

"Don't count on it," Lottie said seriously. "It's not like the olden days. The museum has some of the best security in the world. I've heard it's harder to steal a painting there than it is anywhere else in the entire world."

The train lurched forward as it stopped at the next train station. Lottie fell flat on her face and her bag filled with books skittered across the floor.

"Not again," Lottie huffed.

"I'll help you," Lucy said.

She bent down to help her sister pick up her books. Even though Lucy was only three minutes older than Lottie, they were as different as could be. Lottie loved books and reading.

Lucy was crazy about mysteries and being a detective.

As the train car started to leave the station, Lucy yelled down the aisle, "Dad is this our stop?"

"Oh, sorry, I wasn't paying attention. Nope, one more stop to go," said Mr. Parker.

Mr. Parker glanced down at his phone and frowned. "Listen, kids, I've got some bad news. I just got an email that I'm needed across town for a meeting. I'm afraid you guys will have to go to the Museum on your own. I'll meet up with you after lunch."

Lucy's eyes grew wide. Did he mean they'd be spending a whole morning in Paris by themselves, without their dad around?

Mr. Parker handed them three gold passes to hang around their necks. "These badges will get you into the museum for free," he said.

The kids put the passes around their necks, as Mr. Parker handed them each spending money.

"This is for breakfast, and if you need anything else. I want you guys to stick together. And remember, don't touch any of the art. Got it?" Mr. Parker told them.

"Got it," Ollie, Lottie, and Lucy said at the same time.

"Why can't we touch anything?" Lottie asked.

Lucy looked at her sister sideways. "Do you remember that time you touched an eel at the aquarium and you got electrocuted?"

"Your hair stood on end for a week!" Ollie laughed.

"Well, an art museum is just like that," Lucy said.

Lottie's eyes grew wide and she couldn't tell if they were joking or not, but she decided not to chance it.

The train car lurched into the next station, and this time, Lottie held on tight. Just as her backpack went flying, she grabbed it out of mid-air. "That was a close one," she whispered.

Mr. Parker jumped out of the train car. As the doors were closing, he said, "Remember to stick together, alright?"

"We will," Ollie and Lucy shouted. Lottie added, "Oui Oui!"

Lucy and Ollie both looked at her funny.

"We we? What does that mean? Do you have to go to the bathroom or something?" Ollie laughed.

Lottie snorted. "No! Oui means yes in French. It's spelled o-u-i, but it's pronounced like we. I've been practicing my French," she said as she pointed to the book in her lap.

"Learn French in Three Days?" Ollie exclaimed. "What day are you on?"

"I'm almost to the end," Lottie said as she snapped the book shut. "You know, speaking French might come in handy. Just wait and see."

Just then, the train dinged as it pulled into the station. "This is it, guys! It's our stop!" Lucy shouted.

Within minutes, Ollie, Lottie, and Lucy walked up to the Louvre Art Museum while Lottie munched on a pastry.

"That looks amazing!" Ollie said as his mouth watered.

"It's called Pain Au Chocolat," Lottie said as she pointed to the phrase in her book. "It's really just a chocolate croissant. But, it sounds better in French. Don't you think?"

"I think it'll sound better when I'm chewing it," Ollie joked.

As they turned the corner, they saw police tape across the entrance to the museum and French police officers asking people questions.

People in the crowd whispered to one another, but it was hard to hear what they were saying.

"We can't understand them because they're

speaking French," Lucy said.

"See, I told you that my little book would come in handy," Lottie smiled.

"Well, don't make us wait. What are they saying?" Ollie begged.

"They're saying that one of the Picasso drawings, worth over a million dollars, has been stolen!" Lottie gasped.

CHAPTER TWO

"A robbery!" Lucy shouted. "Do they know who did it?"

Lottie leaned towards a bunch of grown-ups who were gossiping. "They say they have no idea who did it. The thief got away early this morning without anyone seeing him."

"Him or *her*," Lucy said. "If nobody saw the robber, they don't know if it's a guy or a girl."

"Good point," Lottie said. "Shhh, I want to hear more," she whispered. She leaned her head so far over, she nearly tipped into the bushes.

"What else are they saying?" Ollie asked.

"I can't understand much because they're talking so fast," Lottie said as she craned her neck. "The only word I understand is mystery."

"You know what I'm thinking?" Lucy beamed.

"Oh no, not again," Ollie laughed. "We're not getting caught up in solving another one of your detective cases. Are we?"

"I can't help it if we're the best at solving cases," Lucy smiled.

"Oh boy, here we go," Ollie sighed.

"Ollie's right," said Lottie. "This seems pretty serious. Maybe we should leave this one to the police to solve."

The kids looked out at the open courtyard as police detectives searched the area. The police officers wore black uniforms with shiny black boots. They wore hard caps on their heads and carried long sticks in their back pockets.

"Well, if the museum is closed, what should we do instead?" Ollie asked. "We aren't meeting up with Dad for hours."

"Notre Dame Cathedral isn't too far. We could walk along the Seine River, which is right down this hill," Lottie said as she pointed across the courtyard.

Just then, a police officer walked up to the kids. His uniform was black with shiny gold buttons. His black boots were scuffed with faint brown marks across the tops.

"Excuse moi," the Officer began.

"Oh, we don't speak French," Lucy said quickly.

"Je parle un petit peu," Lottie added. "It means, I speak a little French," she whispered to Ollie and Lucy.

"In that case, allow me to practice my English," the officer said in a French accent.

"My name is Detective Percy and I work for the Paris Police Department." He smiled warmly at the kids as he pulled a piece of paper from his pocket.

"Have you seen this person?" Detective Percy asked as he showed the kids a hand-drawn sketch of a teenage girl. She was wearing a yellow scarf with bright fringe around her neck. Her hair was blonde and long, pulled back into a neat ponytail.

"Nope, we haven't seen her before," Ollie replied.

"That's a great drawing," Lottie said as she pointed to the sketch of the girl.

"Thanks, I drew it myself," Detective Percy said as his cheeks turned pink. His hands had pencil markings on them, and little flecks of paint dotted his face.

Detective Percy ran his fingers across the drawing. "You're sure you haven't seen this girl anywhere?" he asked.

"I'm sure. We just got here," Ollie told him.

"Very well," Detective Percy said as he

turned to leave.

"Wait a minute, err…excuse moi," Lucy said. "Does this have anything to do with the museum being shut down today?"

Detective Percy turned on his heel. "Why, yes it does, as a matter of fact," he said. "There was a robbery here this morning of a very valuable sketch by Pablo Picasso, the famous artist."

"What happened?" Ollie asked.

"The security cameras were turned off for one minute, and that's when the thief grabbed the art from the wall in the museum," Detective Percy explained.

"What kind of art was it?" Lucy asked as she leaned in closer.

"It was a small drawing on a piece of paper. Picasso drew it when he was a young art student in Paris. In fact, he drew it right in this court-yard. Maybe in the same spot where you're standing right now," Detective Percy said as he pointed to the kids' feet.

"Wow, a piece of paper is worth a million dollars?" Ollie blinked.

"Over a million dollars," Detective Percy nodded.

"And this is the thief who stole it?" Lottie asked looking at the sketch of the girl in the yellow scarf.

"No, it's not that," Detective Percy chuckled. "This girl is the only witness. She was the only person here this morning when the thief stole the painting. I'd need to talk with her to see if she can identify the robber."

"Oh wow," Lucy said. "This sounds like a mystery for the LOL Detective Club."

"The LOL...what?" Detective Percy asked, looking confused.

"Oh, it's just the name of our Detective Club," Ollie said sheepishly. "My sister thinks we're detectives who solve mysteries. My sister's name is Lucy, my name is Ollie, and my other sister is Lottie. If you put the first initial of all our names together, it spells LOL Detective Club."

"Is that so?" Detective Percy said with a wry smile. "In that case, will you please let me know if you solve zee great mystery of the missing girl?"

"You bet," Lucy cheered as she jumped to her feet. "Ollie, take a picture on your tablet of Detective Percy's drawing."

"Great idea," Ollie said as he snapped a picture of the sketch of the girl.

"We'll be sure to let you know if we see the girl in the yellow scarf," Lottie smiled.

Detective Percy put his sketch back in his pocket. Under his hat, a few stray hairs peeked out wildly. He peered through his round black glasses that slid down his sweaty nose.

"I will give you my private phone number to text me should you find zee girl," Detective Percy said quickly. Ollie typed the phone number on his tablet and slid it into his backpack.

When Ollie looked up, Detective Percy had disappeared.

"Where did he go?" Ollie blinked.

"Beats me," said Lucy. "I'm just so excited we have another case to solve!"

"You and your mysteries," Ollie sighed.

"I can't help it if they follow us wherever we go," Lucy beamed.

CHAPTER THREE

"The art was stolen only an hour ago. The girl has got to be around here somewhere," Lucy said as she scanned the crowd. The police had taped off the whole museum courtyard. Most of the tourists had left for the day.

"Well, it doesn't look like she's here," Ollie said. "The police would have found her by now."

Lottie pulled out her Paris Guide Book and opened it to the map in the center. "Look guys, we're never going to find her. And besides, we didn't come to Paris to look for a girl in a scarf. I want to see the Eiffel Tower and Notre Dame Cathedral."

Lucy leaned over Lottie's guide book. "What's Notre Dame Cathedral?" Lucy asked.

"Only one of the most famous Cathedrals in all of Europe," Lottie exclaimed. "It was built in 1163 and took a hundred years to finish."

"A hundred years?" Ollie said. "Let me see this book." He picked the book up and started thumbing through the pages.

Lottie grabbed the book out of Ollie's hands. "Nobody separates me from my books," she giggled. Lottie was crazy about books and carried a stack of them with her wherever she went.

"Geez, calm down," Ollie sighed. "Look at the map. Notre Dame is just a short walk from here. All we have to do is cross the bridge over the Seine River and we're there."

"And then from Notre Dame, we're only a short walk to the Eiffel Tower," Lottie added.

"Alright, but you're going to carry your heavy backpack all by yourself," Ollie sighed as he picked Lottie's backpack off the ground. "What do you have in here, anyway? A stack of bricks?"

"Not bricks! All my precious books," Lottie smiled.

"Come on, you two. Let's start walking. We might see our mystery girl in the yellow scarf on the way," Lucy said.

The kids walked down the sidewalk leading to the Seine. It was a quiet morning. Besides the extra activity from the robbery, everything seemed totally normal.

An old lady in an orange scarf hobbled towards them.

"Is that her? Is that a yellow scarf?" Lucy whispered.

"Are you joking?" Ollie laughed. "That scarf

is bright orange, not yellow. And besides, that lady is probably ninety years old. Not a teenager."

A family with two little kids in a stroller scooted past them.

"Did you see that lady?" Lottie exclaimed. "I think she had a yellow scarf around her neck!"

Lucy looked back. "Good eyes, Lottie. But that's not a scarf, it's just her sweater hanging out from under her coat."

They walked across the Seine River and watched the tourist boats pass underneath the bridge. "She could be anywhere," Lucy sighed. "It's going to take a lot of detective work to find her."

When they reached Notre Dame Cathedral, it was as big as Lottie had imagined it.

"Look at the architecture," she gasped.

"The architecture, what's that?" Lucy asked.

"It means how a building is designed. What it looks like," Lottie said.

"It looks spooky to me," Ollie said as he pointed up to the creepy gargoyles over the towers.

"Spooky and beautiful," Lottie sighed as she hefted her backpack over her shoulder. "These straps are really starting to hurt," she frowned.

Ollie looked over and saw the straps digging into his sister's shoulder.

"Here, let me take that for a bit," Ollie said. He lifted the backpack off Lottie's shoulders and threw it across his back.

"But, you said Lottie needed to carry her own backpack, remember?" Lucy reminded him.

"That's what families do. We help each other out," Ollie smiled. "Now, are you sure there aren't any bricks in here?"

Lucy scanned the courtyard in front of the Cathedral.

"It doesn't look like our mystery girl is here either," she sighed. "Let's keep moving."

"Keep moving?! We just got here," Lottie said. "At least let me take a peek inside the Cathedral."

"Okay, but make sure you keep an eye out for the girl in the yellow scarf. I'll wait out here with Ollie in case she shows up," Lucy added.

Lottie walked inside the huge cathedral. Bright stained glass windows hung on the walls overhead. The ceiling seemed at least a thousand feet tall. She had never felt so small in her whole life. She looked around, but didn't see a blonde haired girl anywhere. Just some old people and a few babies.

Out in the courtyard, Ollie leaned back on a fence post.

"One thing's been bugging me," he said.

"What's that?" asked Lucy.

"How did Detective Percy know the girl was there if the cameras were turned off and she was the only witness?"

"What do you mean?" Lucy said.

"It's just that if someone was there to see the girl in the yellow scarf, there would have been two witnesses. Who told the police about the girl in the yellow scarf?" Ollie wondered.

"I don't know. Maybe a security guard or a janitor saw her," Lucy said.

Just then, Lottie strolled back into the courtyard.

"Did you see a girl fitting the description?" Lucy asked as soon as she saw her sister.

"Nope, not a single one. It was pretty dark in there, so I might have missed somebody but I don't think so," Lottie said.

"Next time bring a flashlight instead of so many books," Ollie joked.

Lottie brushed her dark hair out of her eyes as she squinted at her brother.

"I'm just kidding," Ollie said as he patted his sister on the shoulder.

CHAPTER FOUR

The air turned chilly and it started to rain as the kids left Notre Dame Cathedral. They walked along the muddy path next to the Seine River.

A few minutes later they arrived at the Eiffel Tower. In front of the Eiffel Tower, a long grassy park stretched past a colorful carousel. A few little kids rode the wooden ponies as the rain drizzled overhead. Just then, the rain stopped and the sun peeked out from behind a cloud.

"Look guys, a rainbow!" Lucy shouted. Across the top of the Eiffel Tower, a rainbow stretched from one side to the other.

Ollie grabbed his tablet from his backpack and snapped a picture. "This will be perfect for my blog," he said.

The three kids walked up to the Eiffel Tower and waited in line for the elevator to the top.

Lucy whispered to Ollie, "Hey, can I see that picture on your tablet of the girl in the yellow scarf again? I don't want to forget what she looks like."

Ollie passed the tablet to Lucy, who studied the picture carefully. Just then, her face lit up.

"Guys, save my place in line. I'm going to check the gift shop and see if they sell yellow scarves. Maybe the girl bought her scarf here and they remember her," Lucy said.

Lucy ran off to the gift shop around the corner as Ollie called back to her, "Don't take forever or you'll miss the elevator."

"If I miss it, I'll take the stairs," Lucy shouted back. Ollie looked up and gulped. The Eiffel Tower was about a million stories tall.

"I don't even want to think about how many stairs that is," he groaned.

Lucy ran into the gift shop and raced right up to the cashier. "Excuse me, ma'am. Do you sell yellow scarves?" Lucy blurted out.

The woman looked at her funny. It dawned on Lucy that the woman spoke only French.

"Oh, if only Lottie was here to translate," Lucy grumbled.

She looked out in the hallway just in time to see the elevator doors opening. The bell dinged as a line of people hopped onto the elevator.

"Well, in any case, ummmm…excuse moi," Lucy said.

She tried her best to explain that she was looking for a girl in a yellow scarf, but nothing made sense. She jumped up and down and pointed. The more she jumped up and down, the more confused the lady behind the counter looked.

Ollie walked around the corner. "You look like a monkey jumping up and down like that!" he laughed.

"I thought you guys got on the elevator," Lucy said.

"We wouldn't leave you," Lottie said as she grabbed her twin sister's hand. "Besides another elevator comes along every few minutes. Or we can take the stairs."

"Jumelles!" the woman exclaimed as she looked at Lottie and Lucy.

"Yes, I mean, oui," Lottie smiled.

"Jumelles means twins in French," Lottie whispered to Lucy. Sometimes it was easy to forget that Lottie and Lucy were identical twins since their personalities were so different.

"That's right, you speak French! Thank goodness," Lucy hugged Lottie. "Never have I ever been so happy to have a twin sister."

"Why is that?" Lottie asked, confused.

"I've been trying to find out about the girl in the yellow scarf, but I don't speak a word of French."

"No worries, sis. I've got this," Lottie giggled.

Lottie spoke in French with the woman behind the counter. After a few minutes, Lottie turned back to Lucy and Ollie.

"Well, what did she say? Don't keep us waiting," Lucy begged.

"She says that she's never seen that scarf before. It's not Parisienne, or high Paris fashion. She says it looks like a homemade scarf," Lottie explained.

"Well, did she see the girl?" Lucy asked.

"She said she sees girls like that every day, probably a dozen," Lottie answered.

"So, what were you guys talking about all that time?" Lucy sighed.

"We were laughing at how funny you looked jumping up and down like a monkey," Lottie snorted.

"Well, I'm glad you think it's funny," Lucy giggled.

"Come on, let's start climbing some stairs," Ollie sighed. "We only have a million to go before we get to the top."

By the time the kids reached the top of the Eiffel Tower, they gasped as they looked out over the whole city of Paris.

"Everything looks so tiny from up here," Lottie exclaimed.

"The cars look like toys, and the people look like ants," Ollie said.

"Can you see a girl in a yellow scarf?" Lucy asked as she peered down below.

"Are you crazy? I just said the people look like ants! How many ants do you know who wear yellow scarves?" Ollie laughed.

The buildings were gray and all in a row,

like tiny toy figures lined up across the city of Paris.

"Look, I think I see our hotel from here," Lucy shouted.

"How can you tell? All the buildings look the same," Lottie said. "That could be a restaurant, or a cafe, or a pastry shop, or a…"

"Lottie, I'm noticing a pattern here. Are you hungry?" Ollie snorted.

"I'm so hungry I could eat my shoe!" Lottie panted. "I really worked up an appetite climbing all those stairs."

"Too bad your shoe isn't made of chocolate," Lucy giggled as they headed down the long flights of stairs.

CHAPTER FIVE

"Even the air smells delicious in Paris," Lottie sighed as they walked by the Cafe next to the Louvre Art Museum.

Lucy peeked her head around the corner and spied rows of delicate French pastries in a brightly lit glass case.

"They look so good. I could eat every last one!" Lottie drooled as she dashed inside the small cafe.

The owner of the cafe looked down his nose at the three kids.

"Is this for eating here?" he said in a thick French accent.

"Oui oui," Lottie said excitedly as she pointed to three pastries in the cabinet.

"How are we ever going to find the girl with the scarf?" Lucy sighed. "It makes me almost lose my appetite."

"Good, then I'll just eat yours," Lottie joked.

Suddenly, Ollie took a step back and said nervously, "Um guys, I have something to show you I know you'll want to see."

Lottie and Lucy spun around to look at Ollie. "Is it another thing for your blog, Ollie? Don't forget, we're trying to catch a thief," Lucy reminded him.

Lottie's eyes grew big when she saw Ollie pointing to a painting that hung on the wall behind the cafe counter. The painting showed the very same girl that Detective Percy had drawn in his picture.

"That can't be her, can it?" Lottie gasped.

"Look, even her scarf is the same," Lucy said as she pointed to the long yellow scarf with the colorful fringe. In the painting, the girl's long blonde hair hung in a neat ponytail and her bright blue eyes stared back at them.

"Looks like we found a clue, finally!" Lucy exhaled.

"Excuse moi," Ollie said to the man behind the counter. Ollie noticed the man's nametag said Hugo, and that he was as tall as a giraffe. "Can you tell me who's in this painting, and if we can talk to the artist who painted her?"

"You can talk to both," Hugo chuckled as he towered over Ollie. "Zee artist and zee girl are zee same person. It is a self-portrait of Sofia Simon."

"Oh, really," Lucy jumped up. "Well, do you know where we could find Sofia Simon?"

"Sofia works here. She's an art student, too. I let her hang her paintings up in the cafe to sell. Do you want to buy one?" Hugo said.

"Err...not exactly," Ollie said slowly. "I'm writing a story for my blog, and I'd love to interview her. When will she be here next?"

"Any minute," Hugo said. "She should be here now. She's running late, which is odd because she's never late."

Lucy looked at Ollie suspiciously. "I hope she's not in any trouble," Lucy whispered.

The kids took a seat at a table in the corner and dug into their pastries and hot chocolate.

"LOL Detective Team huddle," Lucy whispered as they put their heads close together.

"You don't have to say that every time we sit down," Ollie laughed.

"I know," Lucy said. "It just makes us sound more official."

Lottie glanced around the cafe nervously. "Guys, I don't know about this. Something tells me this girl is in more trouble than we thought. Why is she late for work?"

"Yea, what if she's the one who stole the Picasso drawing? She *is* an art student. Maybe she wants to sell it for money, so she doesn't have to work here anymore," Ollie said.

"Why wouldn't she want to work here?" Lottie gasped. "All the desserts you can eat. They could just pay me in chocolate," she sighed.

"Oh Lottie," Lucy giggled. "Detective Percy said this girl saw the crime, not that she did the crime."

"But what if she's got something to do with stealing the art and the cops aren't telling us?" Ollie wondered.

"I guess we'll know in a minute when she gets here," Lucy said excitedly.

"Unless the robber already found her and he's holding her hostage. Maybe that's why she's late to work," Lottie said.

CHAPTER SIX

The kids ate their pastries in silence. They were thinking about the girl in the yellow scarf and if she'd really been kidnapped.

They were daydreaming so much, they didn't notice when a girl with long blonde hair shuffled through the front door. She tied an apron around her waist and began sweeping behind the counter.

Ollie jumped up when he heard the cash register ding. "Is that Sofia Simon?" he asked.

Lottie and Lucy looked across the counter at the girl with the long blonde hair. She had stuffed her hair up into a baseball cap, and she wasn't wearing a scarf. Her big blue eyes peeked out from underneath the hat's brim.

"It's definitely her, alright," Lucy said. "And look, I can see the scarf hiding inside her backpack."

The girl's paint splattered backpack hung on a hook on the wall behind the counter. In the front pocket, you could see her phone and some scarf fringe through the mesh pocket. Ollie scooted his chair back from the table and walked over to the counter.

"Excuse moi, are you Sofia Simon?" Ollie asked.

"Yes, I am," Sofia said nervously as she glanced around the cafe.

"I was wondering if we could ask you a few questions?" Ollie replied, hopefully.

"About the cafe? What would you like to

eat? We have pastries, crepes, and hot choco-late," Sofia said as she pointed to the desserts in the display case.

"Not exactly. See, we've already eaten," Ollie said as he wiped the crumbs from his mouth.

Lucy stepped up to the counter beside her brother. "It's about the robbery over at the Art Museum," Lucy blurted out.

"Could we, um, speak to you in private?" Lucy whispered as she pointed to the cafe table where Lottie sat nibbling every last crumb of her muffin.

"I don't know anything about that," Sofia said as she looked down at her feet.

"The police say that you saw the thief escape this morning. They need to talk to you to see if you know who he is," Lucy told her.

"But, that's impossible," Sofia replied. "The courtyard was completely empty this morning when I saw the thief run out of the building. By the time the security guards came, I had already hidden behind the bushes."

"Well, there must have been somebody, like a janitor, who saw you," Ollie explained. "The police have a sketch of you and everything." Ollie pulled out his tablet and showed Sofia the picture he had taken of Detective Percy's sketch.

"That does look like me," she said quietly. "This drawing looks like it was done in a hurry because it's a little bit smeared. But other than that, it's not bad."

"So, will you talk to us?" Lucy pleaded.

Sofia nodded her head and smiled thinly. "Sure, I'll answer a few questions. But then I've got to get back to work, okay?"

"You got it," Lucy and Ollie said at the same time. Sofia took off her apron and sat down next to Lottie at the table.

"Why don't you start at the beginning?" Ollie said as he sipped the last of his hot chocolate.

"Well, I was at the Art Museum this morning. I always go there at sunrise before my shift at the cafe starts. I love to sketch in the courtyard when it's empty, just like Picasso used to do when he was an art student," Sofia explained.

"You're an art student like Picasso? Maybe you'll be as famous as him one day," Lottie said excitedly.

"I doubt it," Sofia sighed. "I want to be a professional artist and have my own art gallery. But, Paris has so many amazing artists, it's hard to get noticed. Hugo lets me sell my paintings here in the cafe. But so far, nobody's bought even one lousy painting."

Lottie, Ollie, and Lucy frowned. "I bet you'll sell one soon," Lucy said hopefully.

"It's okay," Sofia smiled. "I just hope that one day my paintings sell as fast as Hugo's chocolate muffins."

"In that case, I'll buy a dozen," Lottie said

dreamily.

"Guys, let's get back to the robbery. We have a mystery to solve," Lucy reminded them cheerfully. "Sofia, you said that you were in the courtyard at the Louvre this morning at sunrise?"

"Right, I was the only person in the courtyard. The sun was rising and the beautiful pyramid next to the museum was lit up like a sparkling diamond," Sofia said. "It was so beautiful, I had to take a video of it on my phone. Just as I hit record, a man with a ponytail came running out of the museum clutching a piece of paper."

"I'll bet that was the stolen Picasso sketch!" Lucy said as slapped her hand on the table. The drinks shook and almost spilled as the table wobbled back and forth.

"I guess it was the Picasso sketch, but I didn't know that at the time. The thief stuffed the piece of paper into the back pocket of his pants. As he ran past me, he looked straight into my eyes and I know he saw me," Sofia whispered. Her lower lip trembled as if she was about to cry.

"Then what happened?" Ollie asked as he scooted his chair closer.

"The alarms started blaring so loudly my ears popped. And then a few seconds later, a bunch of security guards ran out of the building," Sofia said. Her fingers drummed nervously in her lap, as if she had something else to tell them but was too afraid.

"What did you do after the alarms went off?" Lucy asked.

"I didn't know what to do! I was afraid the thief would catch me, so I have been hiding out all morning. I went inside Notre Dame Cathedral to think of what to do next," Sofia whispered.

"We were at Notre Dame an hour ago looking for you," Lottie squeaked. "It was so dark in there. I must have missed you."

"I thought the quiet of the Cathedral would help me think, but I still don't know what to do. What do you think the police want with me?" Sofia asked.

"Well, Detective Percy said that you could identify the thief. That Picasso sketch the robber stole is worth a million dollars," Ollie said.

"Over a million dollars," Lottie corrected him.

"But, if I go to the police and they don't catch the thief, he'll be sure to find me. He might even want to hurt me if he finds out I've been talking to the police," Sofia said. Her voice trembled and her eyes welled with tears.

"Listen, I know a thing or two about being scared," Lucy said. "But being scared doesn't mean you can hide from what's right. Being brave means doing the right thing even when it scares you."

"I guess you're right," Sofia said. "It would be a shame for the robber to get away with stealing a million dollar drawing just because I was too afraid to talk to the police."

"So you'll meet with Detective Percy?" Lucy asked.

"Sure, just promise me you guys will come with me when I meet him," Sofia said as she dabbed her wet eyes with her napkin.

"We wouldn't miss it for the world," Lucy beamed. "We're a detective club. Solving mysteries is what we do best."

CHAPTER SEVEN

Sofia grabbed her phone and texted Detective Percy's phone number Ollie had saved on his tablet.

"What did you tell Detective Percy?" Ollie asked.

"I just said that I wanted to meet with him. Oh, and I told him about the video I took of the robber," Sofia answered.

After a few minutes, Sofia's phone beeped back. Lucy grabbed the phone and started to read what Detective Percy had written.

"What does it say?" Lottie and Ollie asked. "I'm almost too afraid to find out," Sofia squeaked.

"Detective Percy said to meet him at the courtyard of the Art Museum in twenty minutes. He said to bring the video and not to watch it or tell anyone else about it. He says it's a matter of official police business," Lucy read from Sofia's phone.

"What does that mean?" Lottie asked, puzzled.

"I dunno. Maybe it means that if the video gets out, it could fall into the wrong hands," Lucy guessed.

"Well, that makes me want to watch the video now," Ollie joked as he wiped the crumbs from the table.

"I'm going out for a bit. I'll be back soon," Sofia called to Hugo as they all walked out of the cafe. Lottie scooped up another chocolate muffin as they headed out the door.

"Lottie, do you ever stop eating?" Ollie teased his sister.

"What? I might get hungry on the way," Lottie laughed.

"The courtyard is right there," Ollie said as he pointed to the stone walkway just a few feet away.

"It's always best to be prepared," Lottie smiled as she took another bite of the delicious pastry.

"Detective Percy said he'd meet us on the bench over by the glass pyramid," Sofia said. She pointed to the courtyard, which was still pretty empty except for a few tourists wandering around the gardens.

"Something about this just doesn't sit right with me," Ollie said slowly.

"You're making me so nervous, my stomach is doing flip flops," Sofia gulped. "What if the thief is watching us right now?" she shivered.

"That's impossible," Lottie reasoned. "Why would the thief come back to the scene of the crime? This place is crawling with police officers."

"Maybe so, but sometimes the safest place to hide something is in plain sight," Lucy said. "Do you remember that time dad hid all my birthday presents under a pile of laundry in my bedroom? We looked all over the house, but nobody thought to look under the stinky socks."

"I remember that," Lottie said. "I think Dad was trying to get you to clean your room," she laughed.

"Uh huh," Ollie muttered under his breath. His nose was pressed against his tablet, and he wasn't paying attention.

"Earth to Ollie! Why are you playing games on your tablet? You're supposed to be helping us keep a lookout," Lucy huffed.

"No, I wasn't playing games. I was, um, working on my blog." Ollie furrowed his eyebrows and glanced at his tablet curiously, as if he was working something out in his head.

"Let me see," Lucy said as she grabbed the tablet. "Ollie, you're not working on your blog. You're watching Sofia's video of the robbery."

"Yea, I copied it from her phone to my tablet back when we were in the cafe," Ollie said sheepishly. "I was curious. And besides, it's always good to have a backup."

"But, Detective Percy said not to show the video to anyone. I'm sure that included making a backup copy on your tablet," Lucy scolded him.

"Well, I didn't know that when I copied it. Besides, I'm not going to show anybody else," Ollie said. Lucy wasn't satisfied and crossed her arms across her chest.

"Look, I'll delete it once I'm done watching it. Deal?" Ollie promised.

"It's a deal. But, since you have it open, let me see it, too," Lucy whispered as she leaned in close.

"Go back to the beginning," Lottie said as she peered over their shoulders.

The video started the same way Sofia had told them the story back at the cafe. The light danced across the beautiful glass pyramid in the courtyard of the Art Museum. Then, a man came running out of the building clutching the Picasso drawing. He stuffed the drawing into the back pocket of his pants. Suddenly, a gust of wind flew across the courtyard and threw his gray hoodie off his head for a second. His long ponytail whipped out from under his hood.

"Something seems strange about that guy," Ollie puzzled.

"Freeze frame right…there," Lucy said as she stopped the video on the man's face.

"What is it about him?" Lottie whispered. "I think I've seen him somewhere before."

Just then, Detective Percy walked up to the kids. Ollie stuffed his tablet back into his backpack.

"You're going to delete the video, right?" Lucy whispered into Ollie's ear.

"Yea, deleting it right now," Ollie said as he pressed a button on his screen and tossed his tablet back into his backpack.

CHAPTER EIGHT

"How wonderful, I see you're all here," Detective Percy smiled as he looked through his round spectacles at the kids. "I guess I have the LOL Detective Club to thank for finding our most important witness."

"Well, your sketch helped us find Sofia," Lucy beamed. "There are only so many yellow scarves in Paris. It was just good old fashioned detective work and a little luck," she boasted.

"Yes, good old fashioned detective work,"

Detective Percy chuckled. "Now, if you please, I would like to see the video you took of zee robber," he insisted.

"It's right here," Sofia said as she handed Detective Percy her phone.

Sofia's phone skittered from her hands and dropped right on top of Detective Percy's black boot. When he picked the phone up, it was covered in black shoe polish. The spot where the phone had fallen had rubbed the shoe polish off his boots, uncovering their original brown leather.

Lucy remembered that the other police officers had been wearing shiny black boots, not brown boots. Detective Percy's boots had been quickly covered in black shoe polish and hadn't even had time to dry. But, she couldn't figure out why.

Detective Percy reached down to pick up the phone and as he did, a wiry ponytail peeked out from underneath his black police hat.

"Eeeeek!" Lottie, Lucy and Ollie all screamed at the same time.

"I know where I've seen you before," Lucy shouted. "You're the...you're the..."

"Thief from the video!" Lottie yelled as she finished her sister's sentence.

"Clever girls," Detective Percy sneered as his lips formed a wicked grin.

"Too bad you're already too late for it to matter," Detective Percy said as he snatched Sofia's phone. "I'm taking this video because it's the only proof there is of the robbery. And if you tell anyone about me, I promise you'll regret it."

"Give me back my phone!" Sofia hollered. By the time the words left her mouth, Detective Percy had bolted out of sight down the stone path across the courtyard.

"Follow that man!" Lucy yelled as she raced to catch Detective Percy.

"Lucy, what are you doing? Are you crazy?"

Ollie, Lottie, and Sofia yelled as they ran to catch up with her.

Lucy ran past the police officers waiting outside the Art Museum.

"The Picasso art thief is headed this way. Follow me," she shouted breathlessly.

Two police officers took off running behind Lucy as another officer called headquarters over his walkie-talkie.

Detective Percy, who was really Thief Percy, raced straight past the Art Museum and into the garden on the other side of the museum.

Lucy and the real police officers ran faster, with Ollie, Lottie, and Sofia following close behind them. Just when they had almost caught Thief Percy, he disappeared into thin air.

Lucy tiptoed into the garden and peeked around the corner of a row of leafy green bushes. She saw the shiny metal from one of Percy's fake police uniform buttons glimmering in the sunlight. The thief was hiding behind the bushes, catching his breath, when he spotted Lucy staring at him.

"He's right here," Lucy shouted to the Police, who sprinted towards the bushes where the thief was hiding out.

When Percy realized that he was about to be caught by the Police, he dashed from his hiding spot. He raced across the busy street, swerving between cars as they sped through traffic. Finally, he leapt up to the top of the bridge crossing the Seine River.

A team of police cars flooded the area and surrounded the bridge on all sides. Percy looked at the cops on both sides of the bridge. Then he looked straight down into the rushing river below him.

"Oh, no! He's not going to do what I think he's going to do. Is he?" Lucy whimpered.

"I think he's going to jump into the..." Ollie said quickly. Before Ollie had the chance to finish his sentence, Percy jumped straight into the Seine River and started swimming. His long ponytail dunked under the water.

"From up here, he looks like a wet cat after a bath," Lottie squinted.

"I think he looks more like a rat," Ollie joked. "A soggy, wet rat."

Everyone started laughing, except for Lucy who was biting her lip.

"Guys, do you know what this means?" Lucy stammered. "He jumped into the river with Sofia's phone in his pocket. That means the phone got soaked, along with everything else."

"And if the phone got soaked, it means it's broken!" Ollie moaned.

"What do you mean it's broken?" Lottie wondered.

"Do you remember that time you dropped dad's phone in the toilet?" Ollie asked.

"Ollie, why are you bringing that up now? I was three years old. I wanted to see if it ended up in the ocean so I flushed it," Lottie explained to Sofia.

"Right. Well, remember what happened? It broke. Dad lost all his pictures on the phone and you had to use a baby potty for a whole year after that," Ollie reminded her.

"Ollie, stop embarrassing me!" Lottie groaned.

"I get what he's saying," Sofia said. "It means that my phone is ruined. And the video of the thief is gone, too!"

CHAPTER NINE

"There goes our evidence!" Lucy cried. "We were this close to catching the thief, and now it's all ruined."

"And my phone is ruined," Sophia sulked. "It took me a year to save up for it."

"Well, I can't get your phone back, but the video isn't lost," Ollie said as he pulled his tablet from his backpack.

"What do you mean, Ollie?" Lucy asked.

"Don't be mad, but remember how Percy

said not to show the video to anyone? Something in my gut told me that sounded fishy. So, I never deleted the video. I still have it on my tablet," Ollie admitted.

"Ollie, I can't believe you," Lucy and Lottie cried at the same time.

"Are you mad at me?" Ollie asked nervously.

"Mad, how could we be mad? We could hug you," they cheered as they threw their arms around his neck.

Ollie pointed to the police officers fishing Percy out of the river. The thief was soaked from head to toe. His baggy pants fell down around his ankles showing his underwear as he trudged out of the water.

"Looks like the case is solved," Ollie said as he tossed his tablet into his backpack.

"Well, not exactly," Lucy scratched her head.

"What do you mean? The police caught the thief. As soon as we give them the video, they'll have all the proof they need," Lottie said.

"They still have to find the stolen Picasso drawing. I wonder where the thief hid it," Lucy said.

"I guess we can ask the real police when we give them the video," Ollie said as they walked back towards the museum.

As they walked up to the Art Museum, a crowd started clapping and cheering.

"I wonder who they are clapping for?" Lucy said as she glanced around the courtyard. Just then, one of the police officers ran up to her and shook her hand.

"I'm Captain Lucas Banner," the police officer introduced himself. "Great work, guys. The thief was right under our noses all this time and we never caught him. Thanks to you, our museum is safe again."

"No problem," Ollie smiled. "It was no big deal, really."

"I have one question I have to ask you," Captain Banner said. "How did you know Percy was the thief?"

"Just some good detective work," Lucy beamed. "And the black shoe polish on his boots."

Ollie pulled his tablet out of his backpack and showed Officer Banner the video he'd copied from Sofia's phone. It showed the thief running out of the museum and stuffing the Picasso drawing into his back pocket.

"This is great," Captain Banner smiled. "I'd like a copy of this video. It could be the only evidence we have to prove that Percy stole the drawing from the museum."

Captain Banner pulled Sofia's wet phone from his police bag.

"I believe this belongs to you," he said as he handed her the phone, still dripping with water. "I'm afraid it's broken and there's no chance of fixing it," he said sadly.

"As long as the thief is caught, that's all that matters to me," Sofia told Officer Banner. "I'll just have to sell some paintings so I can buy a new phone," she smiled.

"So, you're an art student?" Officer Banner asked curiously.

"Yes, I am hoping to become a professional artist like Picasso one day," Sofia whispered as her cheeks turned bright red.

"Well, it is Paris. You never know what might happen," Officer Banner winked.

"Guys, I just thought of something," Lucy said. "The video shows Percy stuffing the Picasso drawing into his back pocket. I'll bet when he jumped into the river, the Picasso drawing went straight down with him."

"That priceless work of art is ruined," Lottie cried. "It's as soggy as a wet napkin."

"It's million-dollar fish food!" Ollie gulped.

CHAPTER TEN

The next morning, the kids ate a breakfast of orange juice and muffins in their hotel room while Ollie read on his tablet.

Ollie took a big sip of orange juice, and nearly spit it out. "Guys, you're never going to believe this!" he shouted.

"What is it, Ollie?" Lucy and Lottie said at the same time.

"Do you guys remember Sofia's video? Well, somehow it ended up on YouTube, and it's been watched over a million times already," he gulped.

"Are you serious?" Lucy exclaimed as she scooted next to Ollie.

She played the video again. Sure enough, it was the same as Sofia's video of the ponytailed thief running out of the art museum.

"Look, there's a link to your blog, Ollie," Lottie gasped as she pointed to the screen. "I bet your blog is famous by now," she gushed.

"Do a search and see what comes up," Lucy said excitedly.

"Already on it," Ollie said as he typed *Paris Art Thief* into the search bar on his tablet.

"The Paris Tribune newspaper says that the Picasso Art Thief has been found. All thanks to three young American detectives.

"That's us! What else does it say?" Lottie jumped up and down next to Ollie as he read.

"The video of the thief was recorded by an art student named Sofia Simon who works at the Cafe next to the Louvre Art Museum. The video was shared by an American blogger named Ollie Parker and has been viewed over a million times since yesterday," Ollie read.

"Wait, what? Are they talking about your blog, Ollie?" Lucy shouted.

"Um, I guess so. But I didn't share the video, I promise," Ollie said, looking shocked.

"You must have. Look, the original video is posted on your blog," Lottie said as she pulled up Ollie's website on his tablet.

"I must have accidentally hit the share button on my tablet when I stuffed it back into my bag," Ollie winced. "I was trying to hide the tablet from Percy, I was so nervous," he remembered.

"Uh oh. I hope Captain Banner isn't mad at us," Lucy said quickly.

"I don't think he will be. Look at all these funny videos people made of the robbery," Ollie said as they watched videos other people had uploaded. "This one is a mash-up of Sofia's video with dance music," he laughed.

"Okay, enough videos. Are there any other articles about the robbery?" Lucy asked seriously.

"This one says that Percy is an artist who is wanted for stealing paintings at other museums around Paris," Lottie read.

"I guess this was going to be his big pay day," Ollie said as he scrolled down to another article.

"Too bad for him that didn't work out," Lottie giggled.

"Hey, I have an idea," Lucy said as she brushed her thick brown hair out of her eyes. "Let's go down to the cafe and see if Sofia is working. I still have the spending money Dad gave me yesterday."

"But we already ate," Ollie said as he wiped chocolate muffin crumbs off his tablet.

"Well, I was thinking if we put our money

together, we could buy one of Sofia's paintings. You know, as a way of saying thank you and so she can save up for a new phone."

"Great idea," Lottie said. "Besides, I really want to see the Mona Lisa in person. Maybe we can actually go *inside* the museum this time," Lottie added.

An hour later, the three kids walked up to the cafe. A long line of people crowded around the front door.

Lucy stood on a nearby bench and waved to Sofia, who was working inside the cafe. Sofia took off her apron and rushed outside, past the long line of people.

"What is going on here?" Lucy asked excitedly. "Yesterday, the cafe was empty. Why is it so crowded now?"

"It's so exciting, you guys," Sofia said, out of breath.

"Slow down," Ollie laughed. "Just start at the beginning."

"Well, the police released my name to the newspapers. And now all these people have come to the cafe to see my artwork. Every painting that was hanging on the wall has been sold. And that's not all, I have orders for more paintings, too," Sofia gushed.

"That's great news! Now you have enough money to replace your phone," Lottie smiled.

Just then, Officer Banner walked up behind Sofia and tapped her on the shoulder.

"Thanks for helping us catch Percy. I wanted to say thanks, so I bought you a new phone," Officer Banner said. He handed Sofia a shiny white phone that glimmered in the sunlight.

"Hey, that's that brand new model," Ollie exclaimed. "Those don't even come out for another month!"

"I know," Officer Banner said. "It's the least I could do. Who knows, maybe you'll use it to help me catch another thief," he joked.

"Thanks for the phone, Officer Banner," Sofia smiled. She looked back at the crowd gathering outside the cafe. The line had grown twice as long since she'd been standing there talking.

"Listen guys, I've got to go. Thanks for everything," Sofia said as she hugged Lottie, Ollie, and Lucy.

"Sofia, just remember us when you're as famous as Picasso, okay?" Ollie said.

"I could never forget my American friends in the LOL Detective Club," she winked.

Officer Banner's police walkie-talkie beeped. He picked it up and listened to the voice on the other end of the line speaking French.

"I'm sorry, guys. I have to run," Officer Banner said quickly. "My search team found the Picasso drawing. It didn't fall into the river, after all."

"Where was it?" Lucy asked, wide-eyed.

"It was near the bushes next to the river. It must have fallen out when Percy was running.

It flew into a garbage can," Officer Banner said.

"A million dollars in the trash," Ollie laughed. "Why don't I find garbage like that?"

Officer Banner waved goodbye and hurried across the courtyard. When he was just out of sight, Lucy felt someone squeeze her from behind. She turned around and saw their Dad with a bag of freshly baked croissants from the cafe.

"Dad! I thought you were busy all day photographing the event," Lucy said as she gave her dad a hug.

"I so felt bad about my meeting yesterday that I took the whole day off today. You guys must have been bored to tears waiting around for me," he sighed.

"I wouldn't say we were bored, Dad," Lottie giggled.

Ollie and Lucy started laughing so hard that their sides hurt.

"That's good," Dad said. "I would hate to

think my kids weren't having any fun in Paris while I had to work."

"Oh, we kept ourselves busy," Lucy smiled as they all walked into the Art Museum and past the Picasso exhibit. Dad pointed to an empty wall where the stolen drawing was missing.

"Hey, did you guys hear about the Picasso thief?" Dad asked.

"Oh, did we ever," Ollie said, as they all giggled under their breaths.

The End.

Thank you so much for reading *The Paris Puzzler: LOL Detective Club, Book Two.*

If you enjoyed this book, please leave a review on Amazon! I love hearing what my readers think!

Other Books in the Series:
THE MARDI GRAS MYSTERY:
LOL DETECTIVE CLUB BOOK #1

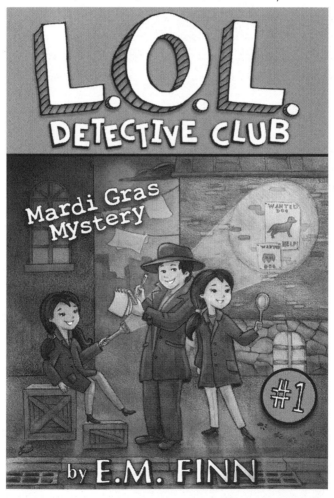

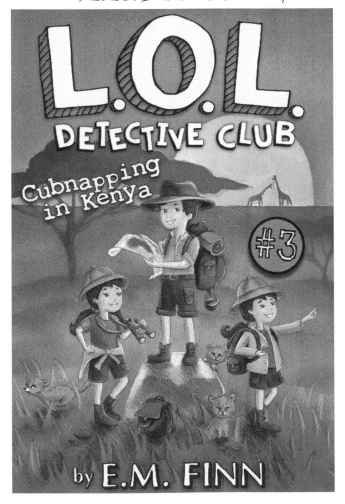

And more coming soon!

Here is a sneak peek of the next book in the
LOL Detective Club Series:

CUBNAPPING IN KENYA
LOL DETECTIVE CLUB BOOK #3

CHAPTER ONE

"I'm so excited to sleep under the stars," Lucy Parker said as she laid her sleeping bag across the wooden floor high up in the trees. Underneath her feet, a giraffe chomped on the leaves that hung below their tree house.

"I just hope a giraffe doesn't lick our feet," Ollie laughed.

"I bet their tongues are like sandpaper. Blech," said Lottie.

The kids were staying in a tree house at the

Safari Wild Animal Park in Kenya, which was a nature preserve on the African plains. At Safari Park, animals like elephants and zebras roamed freely. The best part about Safari Park was that you could sleep in a tree house right alongside the animals. Safari Park also had a plush hotel for guests who liked hot showers and no chance of giraffes visiting them in the middle of the night.

Justin Parker, their dad, traveled the world as a photojournalist and he often took his kids with him on assignment. This time they had travelled to Kenya, a small East African country which is home to animals like elephants, zebras, and lions. Their dad had been sent to photograph the newborn Saharan Cheetah cubs who had just been born at Safari Park. Saharan Cheetahs are one of the most endangered animals in the world, with only a few hundred left in the wild.

Mika, the park's resident Saharan Cheetah,

had surprised everyone by giving birth to three baby cubs just a few weeks ago.

"I can't believe we get to pet a real cheetah," Lucy said.

Lucy was crazy about animals. She hoped to be a veterinarian when she grew up. That is, if being a detective didn't work out.

Lucy had started the LOL Detective Club with her big brother, Ollie, and her identical twin sister, Lottie. Ollie was ten years old and loved computers. Lucy and Lottie were both eight and a half years old. Lucy was three minutes older than Lottie, which made her the older, wiser sister. Or at least that's what Lucy told Lottie every chance she got.

"When do we get to see Mika and her cubs?" Lottie asked their Dad.

"They're introducing the cubs in just a few minutes," Dad said as he gathered up his photography equipment. "There will be quite a few reporters, plus guests from the hotel. Saharan

Cheetahs are critically endangered, which means they are very rare."

The kids walked with their dad over to Cheetah Hill, where Mika lived with her baby cubs. A crowd had already started to gather when a plump man with red cheeks and white hair began speaking over the small crowd that had gathered.

"Hi everybody," he began. "My name is Garth Mabel and I'm the owner of Safari Park. I started this animal preserve twenty years ago. My dream was to build a place where families could come visit animals in a wild habitat. We started with just three animals, and now we've grown to two hundred. Or, two hundred and three if you count Mika's cubs," he smiled.

Ollie hit record on his tablet. "I've got to take a video of this for my blog," he said. "This is the coolest place ever!"

"I can't see," Lottie said as she stood on her tiptoes, trying to look over the heads of all the grown-ups in the front of the crowd.

"Let's stand on this rock," Lucy said. Ollie, Lottie, and Lucy climbed on top of a huge boulder that overlooked the cheetah's grassy den.

"We have the best view from up here," Lottie said.

Dad looked up at the kids sitting on top of the giant rock. "Guys, I have to get up in front of the crowd to take photos. I'll see you back at the tree house later this afternoon," he said.

"Great, dad. Don't get too close to that cheetah. She might eat you," Lottie joked.

Garth kept talking about Safari Park. Ollie wished he'd hurry up so they could see Mika, the cheetah. Just when it looked like Garth was done talking, he turned to a tall lady with cheetah print boots.

"Hello, everyone," the woman drawled. "As most of you know, I am Zoey Zelantia, the heiress to the Zelantia Empire."

The crowd members began to whisper. Everyone knew that the Zelantias had made a lot of money back in the 1800s when they mined for diamonds in South Africa. They had been living off their riches ever since. Zoey Zelantia was known for partying and made frequent appearances in the gossip newspapers.

"My grandfather loved animals. That's why he decided to donate so much money to keep Safari Park's doors open. Without my grandfather, Safari Park would be kaput," Zoey said as Garth coughed quickly.

"Thank you so much, Ms. Zelantia," Garth said as he cleared his throat. The two people standing next to Garth started to fidget nervously. They were both wearing official Safari Park uniforms.

"Who are they?" Lucy whispered.

"Oh, I saw them earlier on the Safari Park website," Lottie said. "The short guy with blue hair is Artie Mack. He takes care of the animals. Feeds them and stuff. The tall woman with glasses is Dr. Linka Long. She's a veterinarian. She's the one who helped Mika deliver her cubs."

"I wish I could have been there when Mika delivered her cubs. That sounds..." Lucy whispered.

"Gross? Slimy?" Ollie said.

"No, Ollie. I was going to say it sounds amazing. I hope I can be a veterinarian one day," Lucy sighed.

"I thought you wanted to be a detective," Ollie said.

"A detective and a veterinarian," Lucy nodded. "Maybe I'll solve animal mysteries."

"Whoever heard of an animal mystery?" Ollie snorted.

"Shhh! I'm trying to hear what they're saying," Lottie whispered.

After Zoey Zelantia finished speaking, Garth introduced Artie Mack. Artie was so short, he looked more like a kid than a grown-up. His voice was high-pitched and squeaked when he talked.

"It's been a real pleasure helping Mika take care of her cubs. They're only three weeks old, so they're with their mom all the time. I make sure Mika's got food and water, and then she takes care of all the rest. They're nursing, so all they do is sleep and eat all day."

"That sounds like a good life to me," Garth chuckled. "Dr. Long, would you like to say a few words before we introduce the cubs?"

"If you insist," Dr. Long blushed. "Can I say what an honor it's been to deliver these beautiful baby cheetahs into the world? With only a few Saharan Cheetahs still alive today, we are so lucky to have a few of them here at Safari Park. These cheetahs are priceless. And cute."

"So cute," Garth beamed. "Without further ado, let's introduce Mika's cubs. Shall we? Artie, would you do us the honors and bring the cubs out to meet the press?"

From inside the grassy den, two large green eyes peered out from the darkness. Then, a gold and black face crept forward with her head low. Her eyes looked drowsy, as if she had just awoken from a long slumber. Long black tear marks ran down her face from the insides of her eyes.

"Is there something wrong with her?" Lucy whispered. "She looks upset."

"Those marks on Mika's face aren't tears. All cheetahs have those black lines by their eyes," Ollie whispered.

"Still, she seems mad," Lucy said.

"Is it safe for Artie to walk up to a cheetah like that? Won't she attack him?" Ollie asked.

"Nope. She won't hurt him. I read on the website that Mika has been at Safari Park since she was a tiny cub. So, she's used to humans," Lottie said.

Artie walked slowly towards Mika. He

reached his hand towards Mika, and she sniffed it slowly. Then, she lifted her nostrils into the wind and smelled the air around her. As Artie reached out to pet her, Mika charged past him and jumped into the crowd of reporters. She snarled as she whipped her tail and bared her teeth.

The reporters in the crowd screamed and ran. They jumped into their jeeps and rolled up the windows tight. Mika pawed at the ground, and sniffed the air as her nostrils flared.

"Dr. Long, I need help!" Artie yelled as he backed away from Mika.

The veterinarian grabbed a dart gun out of her medical bag and walked slowly towards the cheetah.

"She's not going to hurt Mika, is she?" Lucy said as her lip trembled.

"Of course not," Ollie said. "She's going to put her to sleep, I bet."

Within seconds, Mika was fast asleep in a

patch of warm sun. Dr. Long held Mika's head and patted her behind her ears. She whispered something to Mika, but the kids couldn't hear what she said.

"Folks, that was exciting," Garth said to the crowd who'd started to gather at Cheetah Hill. "Mika's fine. She'll be sleeping for a little while, so why don't you all go back to the hotel and grab a bite to eat at the restaurant? We've got a nice special today."

Garth let out a long sigh, and the crowd started to leave. Artie walked back to Mika's den where she had been napping with her cubs earlier. A second later, he ran out of the tall grass yelling and waving his arms.

"Mika's babies are gone. All three cubs have been kidnapped," Artie screamed.

Garth's eyes got huge and his skin turned bright red.

"There must be some mistake," Garth gasped.

"I'm afraid not. Look, whoever did it left a ransom note," Artie said as he handed Garth a thin piece of paper.

"They've been Cubnapped!" Lottie shouted.

About The Author

E.M. Finn writes children's books, including *The LOL Detective Club Mystery Series*.

She lives in Los Angeles with her husband, four daughters, and a goldendoodle named Daisy. Born and raised in Indiana, she moved to California after college and went on to graduate school at USC and UC-Berkeley.

You can find her on her author website, EMFinn.com, and blogging at UrthMama.com, where she has been writing for a decade about the adventures of raising her four girls. When she's not typing away furiously at the keyboard, she homeschools her four young children and encourages her husband in his film and television career.

Some of her favorite children's books include the *Harry Potter* series, *Nancy Drew Mysteries*, *The Boxcar Children*, and the *Little House on the Prairie* books.

Made in the USA
Middletown, DE
19 July 2023